This book is dedicated to the memory of our beloved family cat Winston, whose antics brought us great joy and happiness.

Look for him in this book!

Written by Karla Mansell
With illustrations by her son, Jeremy Mansell

Late one summer afternoon, Simon's family pulled into the driveway of their new house.

Simon pouted and refused to get out of the car. He didn't want to move, but he didn't have a choice once his dad started a new job in Michigan. "We are going in the house right now," his dad said sternly, "and you are coming with us!"

Simon followed his parents into the new house. As he walked down the hallway, he glanced into each room without interest. Then he saw a sign on one of the doors that read 'Simon's Room.'

He hesitated, then slowly opened the door and looked around. There were many large boxes piled up. He realized they were filled with his favorite toys and possessions from his old house. He missed his old bedroom. He thought about how he didn't want to move and leave behind his friends and the school that he loved.

He began to feel quite homesick, so he sat down beside a large box to sulk. Simon felt trapped here in his new house. He was mad at his parents for forcing him to leave everything behind! All Simon could think about was how sad and lonely he felt. He realized he was afraid to meet new friends and wondered if he would always feel this way.

Simon's mom peeked her head around the corner and said, "Don't forget to take your box of winter clothes up to the attic before dinner. I ordered a pizza and it should be here soon. I'll open the door for you."

Simon's mom pulled down a rope that was attached to a trapdoor in the ceiling. She unfolded wooden stairs and pulled them forward. Simon was intrigued by this secret hiding place. He thought it might be fun to go up the stairs and explore.

Simon crept up the attic stairs holding tightly to his box. When he reached the top, he saw an old wooden purple chest with a black cat and jack-o-lantern painted on it. "This must be a treasure chest of sorts," he thought. So, he slowly lifted the lid to look inside.

Simon couldn't believe his eyes! The chest was full of Halloween costumes. Simon loved Halloween and dressing up! He rummaged through the costumes excitedly until he found a superhero costume. Simon paused and thought, "If I were a superhero I would be brave! I wouldn't be afraid of anything!" He quickly put the costume on.

Then he put his hand in his pocket. He felt something strange. He pulled his hand out and found that it was a shiny silver coin with writing on it. The coin read, 'CLOSE YOUR EYES AND MAKE A WISH.'

With the coin in his hand, Simon closed his eyes and made a wish. He said, "I wish it were Halloween today! NO! I wish it were Halloween every day! I would be happy if it were Halloween. I could dress-up every day and be a superhero! I could do whatever I want—like eat candy for breakfast, lunch and dinner!"

Suddenly, the treasure chest started to glow brightly. As Simon put his head inside the chest to look, he felt a force pulling him forward! He began to slide down through the entranceway headfirst! He closed his eyes and felt everything whirling around him as he slowly fell downward...

Then, PLOP! He fell right into a pile of leaves!

As he looked up from the leaf pile, he saw a boy standing next to him. The boy was raking leaves. Simon exclaimed, "Wow! Who are you?" As the boy held out his hand to help Simon up, he said, "I'm Henry, and this is my dog Tricksy. Who are you?"

Simon replied, "I'm Simon. I'm not quite sure how I got here or where I am. But it's nice to meet you!" Henry said, "Well, you are in Halloween Land, where we celebrate Halloween every night. As soon as I finish raking leaves I'm going trick-or-treating. Would you like to go with me? You're already wearing that cool costume."

"Yes, I can't wait!" Simon couldn't believe his wish came true!

Inside Henry's house they got dressed for Halloween. Henry said, "I'm getting my crow costume on, and Tricksy is going to be a scarecrow. We have so much fun dressing up here!"

Simon and Henry joined hands and ran off from house to house collecting candy. As they ran through crunchy leaves, Simon could smell the bonfires burning and feel the crisp cool air of autumn. Halloween had always been Simon's favorite night of the year. He was happy to share it with a new friend.

At one of the houses, Simon met one of Henry's friends—a shy little girl named Lily. She was hiding behind her dad and looking a little sad because no one could take her trick-or-treating. Simon asked, "Would you like to come out with us?" Lily happily agreed and rushed to get her costume on.

Afterward, Simon, Henry, and Lily skipped down the street and collected more candy.

Later in the evening, Henry asked Simon and Lily if they wanted to go to a haunted house. "It's kind of spooky," he explained, "but I heard they have the best candy in the entire neighborhood."

When they got to the house, they stepped onto a creepy porch with spider webs. Enormous chocolate bars were in a bowl on a table. No one was around. As Lily reached for a bar, a witch suddenly jumped out and cackled, "Want some candy little ones?!" Lily screamed, "AHHH!"

Simon picked up Lily and the three of them ran off the porch. They hid behind a bush, scared and empty-handed. Henry puffed, "I didn't want that candy bar anyway!"

At this point, the children's bags were full to the brim with candy so they decided to go home. Simon and Henry walked Lily home before heading back to Henry's house for the night.

Night after night they went trick-or-treating.

Some nights they sorted their candy.

Other nights they carved pumpkins...

One night Simon suggested that they go back to the haunted house. He was confident he could get the best candy in the neighborhood this time!

Henry and Lily were scared, but Simon insisted he would protect them. They all agreed to return to the haunted house.

Once they arrived at the house, they tiptoed onto the porch. Sitting on a table was the bowl of giant chocolate bars. The kids quietly crept up... and each grabbed one! From around the corner, a shadow of the witch appeared! As they ran away they heard her cackle, "Come back with my candy!" They raced down the street until they were out of breath.

They kept running all the way to Henry's house until they saw his mom and dad sitting by a bonfire. Henry's mom said, "Come on over kids! How about roasting some marshmallows?"

At the bonfire, Simon sat next to Lily and sighed. He had been gazing at the fire thinking about his mom and dad and wondering when he would see them again. He said to Lily, "I want to start adventures at my new home, but I'm afraid I won't meet new friends there. Do you think I can still be brave if I'm not a superhero?"

"You are brave, Simon! You don't need the costume to be a hero," Lily replied. "I wouldn't have had all this fun if you hadn't invited me trick-or-treating. You helped me be brave when I was afraid to go to the haunted house. My dad always says, 'Believe in yourself, and you can do anything.'" Simon smiled and said, "Wow! I guess I am brave! How do I get back home though?"

As Simon was speaking, the large chocolate bar from the haunted house started to glow a yellowish color. He opened it up and found a gold coin inside. Just like the silver coin he found, it read, 'CLOSE YOUR EYES AND MAKE A WISH.'

He held the gold coin tightly in his hand as he made the wish to go back home. Suddenly the leaves on the ground glowed brightly. They started to swirl around and form a stairway. At the top of the stairs, he saw the same purple chest he entered to arrive in Halloween Land. He knew it was his way back home.

As he walked up the stairs, he stopped and waved to his friends. "Goodbye! I will miss you!" Then he continued up the stairs and crawled through the chest leading back to the attic of his new house.

Once Simon was back in his attic, he put his superhero costume back into the chest and changed into his clothes. He sighed with relief that he was back home.

Simon could hear his mom calling him down to dinner. He excitedly ran downstairs to the dining room.

He found his mother putting a box of pizza on the table and the movers still bringing boxes into the home. Simon realized that no time had passed when he was in Halloween Land!

His Mom said, "That was quick! Did you already put your box in the attic?" Simon exclaimed, "Yes I did! I'm glad we're having my favorite food for dinner tonight!"

As Simon ate his last bite of pizza, the doorbell rang. He got up and opened the door. A boy about his age was standing there with a younger girl. The boy said, "Hi! I'm your new neighbor Carter, and this is my little sister Madelyn. We saw you moving in today. Do you want to play?"

Simon replied, "Sure! If you help me unpack my room we can go outside to play." Carter and Madelyn happily agreed.

As they unpacked the first box, Simon asked Carter and Madelyn, "Hey, do you like dressing up?"

THE END

About the Author

Karla Mansell is an early-childhood educator who resides in Michigan. She is a devoted mother, grandmother, and preschool teacher. Karla's love of storybooks, along with her dream of creating her own, come to life in this imaginative and fun story.

About the Illustrator

Jeremy is an illustrator, photographer, painter, and engineer. Halloween is his favorite holiday. Many of the illustrations in this book were inspired by his childhood memories of Halloween night. See more of his works at www.jeremymansell.com.

Halloween Every Night!

First Edition

Artist Portraits:
Karla by Thomas Faucher
Jeremy by Charles Santora

Made in the USA
Middletown, DE
02 October 2018